We dedicate this to Patrick Frendo-Cumbo. Your love
and courage will forever be an inspiration to us. . . .
And thank you for putting pumpkins in the garden
when the ones we planted didn't grow. ☺
—L.S. & M.S.

For every child who daydreams,
creates, and imagines . . . keep it up!
—S.B.

In the Waves
Text copyright © 2015 by Lennon and Maisy Stella
Based on a song written by Lennon, Maisy, and MaryLynne Stella and Carolyn Dawn Johnson
Illustrations copyright © 2015 by Steve Björkman
ISBN 978-0-06-235939-1

This artist used a dip pen, waterproof India ink, and Winsor & Newton,
Holbein, and Daniel Smith watercolors on Arches 140 lb bright white
cold-press watercolor paper to create the illustrations for this book.
Typography by Rachel Zegar
14 15 16 17 18 SCP 10 9 8 7 6 5 4 3 2 1
❖
First Edition

In the Waves

Written by **Lennon** and **Maisy Stella**
Based on a song by Lennon, Maisy, and
MaryLynne Stella and Carolyn Dawn Johnson

illustrated by **Steve Björkman**

HARPER
An Imprint of HarperCollinsPublishers

I got my ol' flip-flops
And my hat on top
A coat of sunblock
That I almost forgot

Headed for the blue seashore

Got my boogie-oogie boogie board

Mom says, hurry, hurry come on
What could possibly be taking so long?

We say, Mama, we're almost done
Getting all ready for some sister fun

In the waves, in the water
In the waves, in the water

Just use your imagination
You can have a dream vacation

In the waves, in the water
In the waves, in the water

I got a jug of homemade
Lemonade
A bag of shark bait
Yeah, PB&J

The sky is clear and the fishies are near
I got my scooby-doobie scuba gear

Mom says, hurry, hurry come on
What could possibly be taking so long?

We say, Mama, we're almost done
Getting all ready for some sister fun

In the waves, in the water
In the waves, in the water

Just use your imagination
You can have a dream vacation

In the waves, in the water
In the waves, in the water

We'll ride 'em high
We'll touch the sky
Keep your balance on the board
If we try, try, try

Soak up the sun
Have some beachy fun
A little splish-splash for everyone

In the waves, in the water
In the waves, in the water

In the waves, in the water
In the waves, in the water

Mama calls our names
Once again
Says she's tired of waiting
So we better get in

We just laugh
At the fun we'll have

In the bubbly-wubbly bubble bath

Yeah, we're really not
At a beach that's hot

We're just two sisters who pretend a lot

Search-and-Find Fun

This crab appears fourteen times in this book. See if you can find them all.

Meet Lennon & Maisy

Lennon Ray Louise Stella &
Maisy Jude Marion Stella

Tobogganing at their farmhouse in Canada!

Best friends, always together!

Getting silly at the park!

They always loved singing together.

Performing at the Music Scene in Whitby, Ontario;
Lennon was seven and Maisy was three.

Their video "Call Your Girlfriend" has been
seen more than twenty million times.

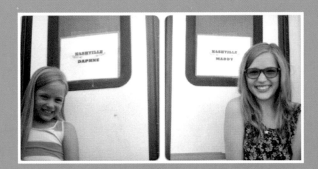

Lennon and Maisy got roles on ABC's hit television
show *Nashville*. This was their first time on set!

Singing at the Grand Ole Opry, June 2013.

The whole Stella family at the White House.